It was the best arcade in town. The video screens shone bright in the big dark room. Seb and Jimmy were lost in the thrill of the games they were playing. The ghosts and aliens seemed real to them.

Then both their screens went dark.

"What's going on?" said Jimmy.

"Don't know," said Seb.

"I turned your games off."

The boys knew the man with the deep voice. He was the arcade owner. He had a bald head and big dark eyes.

"What did you do that for?" asked Seb angrily.

"You play these games very well," said the man. "But are you ready for a real test of skill?"

Chapter 2:
Into Terror World

"What kind of test?" asked Jimmy.

"Yeah," added Seb. "What are you on about?"

"The new Terror World video game," said the arcade owner. "You haven't seen it yet. Nobody has. You can both play it at the same time. Come and check it out."

When Seb and Jimmy saw the new game, they just stood and stared. It had two cool motorbikes and a huge video screen.

Terror World

Tony Norman

Contents

Chapter 1: Start the game   4

Chapter 2: Into Terror World   8

Chapter 3: Razor Cat   14

Chapter 4: Face the fear   21

Chapter 5: Flying high   24

Chapter 6: Go for it!   26

Chapter 7: The end..?   30

Badger
LEARNING

Chapter 1:
Start the game

Jimmy was being chased by ghosts in a dark, scary cave.

Seb was lost in the snow, on a frozen planet.

Jimmy heard the ghosts scream and howl.

Seb saw an army of aliens burst out of an icy sea.

Were they scared?

No. They loved playing the new games in Terror World!

"Neat," said Jimmy.

"Brill," said Seb.

The big, bald man smiled.

"How much does it cost?" asked Seb.

"You can play for free," said the owner. "I want you to try it for me. See what you think."

The boys looked at each other. This was too good to miss.

In no time at all, Seb and Jimmy were on the motorbikes. The man pushed a button. There was a bright flash of light. The boys felt their bikes leap into life. Then, in a rush of speed, they roared into the video screen.

Seb and Jimmy came
out the other side.

They were in Terror World. They raced around the streets of a dark city. High walls of red and black brick rose up to the stormy sky above. Fingers of green light shone from every window. It was the kind of town bad dreams are made of. But Seb and Jimmy loved it.

The roads were smooth, like a race track. Their motorbikes sped along at crazy speeds.

And then, in a flash, it was over.

Jimmy and Seb were back in the arcade.

Chapter 3: Razor Cat

"Well?" asked the arcade owner.

"Top game," said Seb.

"The best," nodded Jimmy.

"There's an even better new game," said the man. "It's called 'Razor Cat', but..."

"But what?" asked Jimmy.

"I think it's a bit too scary for kids like you."

"No way," said Seb.

"Yeah, bring it on," said Jimmy.

"Well," said the man, with an odd smile, "take a look at it first."

The new game had just one motorbike. This time they could see a wild cat moving on the screen. It seemed to be caged behind the glass.

"That's a Razor Cat," said the man. "Scared yet?"

"No," said Seb.

"It's only a game," said Jimmy.

"You've never played a game like this before," said the man.

Seb and Jimmy smiled. They got onto the motorbike.

"Let's do it," said Seb.

"You asked for it," said the arcade owner.

There was a bright flash of light and a huge rush of speed. The boys were back on the mean streets of Terror World. But this time they were on foot.

"Where's our bike?" asked Jimmy.

"Don't know," said Seb, with a shrug.

The two boys walked down the dark street.

"Seems a bit dull this game," said Jimmy.

"Yeah, we can walk down a boring street at home," said Seb.

The boys laughed. Then they heard a mean sound that wiped the smiles off their faces.

"What was that?" asked Jimmy.

"I don't want to find out," replied Seb.

The two friends made a run for it.

The angry roars grew louder. They could hear the scratch of long, sharp claws right behind them. The Razor Cat was closing in fast...

Chapter 4: Face the fear

Jimmy and Seb ran for their lives. "Quick, down here," panted Seb.

They ran into a small side road. Then they froze with fear. They were in a blind alley. There was no way out. They got to the wall at the end of the alley and turned to face the Razor Cat.

It was as big as a lion. It looked just like the picture they had seen on the video screen. But this was for real and now it seemed twice as mean. Tufts of purple hair stuck out of its dry, dusty body. It had blood red eyes and long yellow fangs, like a vampire...

"What a freak!" said Jimmy, in a shaky voice.

"Stay cool," said Seb, trying to think of a way out.

The Razor Cat gave a deep growl and moved closer. Jimmy and Seb edged along the wall.

They felt like rats in a trap. The cat could strike at any time.

Then Seb fell over. Razor Cat made a grab for him, but missed.

Seb jumped to his feet and saw what had made him trip.

"Quick Jimmy," he said, "it's our motorbike. Get on!"

Jimmy did what he was told. Seb kicked the bike into life. He tried to drive out of the alley, but there was no way past the Razor Cat. It rose up on its back legs, with razor sharp claws ready to strike.

Seb shut his eyes...

Chapter 5: Flying high

Lash!

The Razor Cat's huge paw cut through the air like a knife. It missed, but those claws would get them next time for sure. The boys knew they were in real danger.

Then their motorbike took on a life of its own. It gave a loud roar that scared the Razor Cat. The cat jumped back and the bike shot up into the air.

"Hold tight," shouted Seb.

The motorbike flew out of the alley,
leaving Razor Cat alone and angry.

"We're free!" yelled Jimmy.

"Alright!" said Seb. "Now how do we
get out of here?"

Chapter 6: Go for it!

Seb and Jimmy flew high above the streets of Terror World. At first it was a buzz; the best thrill ever. They felt they had won the game for sure. Then they heard the Razor Cat's roar.

Jimmy looked back.

"He can fly!" yelled Jimmy. "He's right behind us."

The boys zoomed out of a long dark street into a big park. What they saw below them made them shake with fear. The park was full of Razor Cats staring at the huge screen of an open-air cinema.

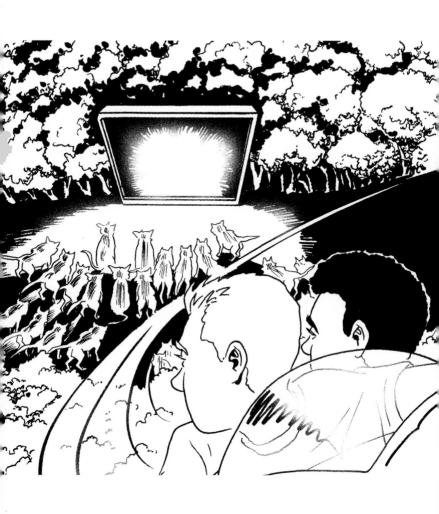

"This can't be for real," said Seb.

"Weird or what?" said Jimmy.

Their bike roared through the sky above the park. When the cats heard the boys above, they looked up and started to roar with rage. The noise they made filled the air. It was like thunder. The cats in the park were ready to fly up and join the Razor Cat from the alley, who was closing in fast.

"What now?" yelled Jimmy.

"Look at the screen," Seb shouted back. "It's the arcade!"

Yes! They could see all the video games they loved to play.

"Let's try and get back!" said Seb.

Jimmy could feel the hot breath of the Razor Cat on his neck.

"Go for it!" he screamed.

Seb flew at the screen. The boys hit it at top speed. There was a flash of light and a loud bang. Then a dark fog seemed to close in all around them.

Chapter 7: The end..?

Seb and Jimmy opened their eyes.

They were back in Terror World. Only this time it was the video game arcade in their home town. The owner was there.

"I need to talk to you," he said.
He seemed very jumpy.

"No way," shouted Jimmy, as he and Seb ran for the exit...

Soon they were walking in a park they knew well. They were both still in shock.

"This place seems so quiet," said Seb.

"Hey, I like it that way," smiled Jimmy.

They were happy to feel safe again.

Then they heard a sound that made their skin go cold.

It sounded like you know who, or were their minds playing tricks on them?

"Maybe it was just the wind in the trees," said Seb.

"It can't be a Razor Cat, can it?" said Jimmy. "I dare you to look back."

"Run for your life!" yelled Seb. And away they ran.

"But the game's over," said Jimmy.

Or was it?